Pitt Street Pirates

by

Terry Deary

Illustrated by Steve Donald

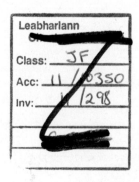
You do not need to read this page – just get on with the book!

First published in 2001 in Great Britain by
Barrington Stoke Ltd
www.barringtonstoke.co.uk

Reprinted 2003 (twice), 2004 (twice), 2005

ISBN 1-842990-05-5

Printed in Great Britain by Bell and Bain Ltd

MEET THE AUTHOR - TERRY DEARY

What is your favourite animal?
A rat
What is your favourite boy's name?
Marmaduke
What is your favourite girl's name?
Bertha
What is your favourite food?
Horse
What is your favourite music?
Bagpipes
What is your favourite hobby?
Singing to bagpipes

MEET THE ILLUSTRATOR - STEVE DONALD

What is your favourite animal?
A goldfish
What is your favourite boy's name?
Kieran
What is your favourite girl's name?
Elizabeth
What is your favourite food?
Scrambled eggs
What is your favourite music?
1970s pop music
What is your favourite hobby?
Playing on my computer

Contents

Before we start ...
Meet the Pitt Street Pirates!

ROGER REDBEARD

Criminal mastermind, Captain of the Pitt Street Pirates, Public Enemy No. 1 and Master of Disguise – calls himself Redbeard yet he does not have a beard! In fact, he's too young to shave – and he never washes behind his ears either ...

Pitt Street Pirates

ELLIE FLYNN

Not quite as big as a gorilla and not quite as pretty – but a lot stronger. This girl is the muscle of the Pitt Street Pirates. Only two weaknesses – chocolate and Roger Redbeard.

SNIFFLE SMITH

The mystery member of the group. Has all the brains of a tin can – an empty tin can. He has even less muscle and he's slower than treacle in a fridge. Only use anyone can think of is for the gang's target practice.

Pitt Street Pirates

MINNIE

Ship's parrot. Possibly the only four-legged parrot in the whole of Pitt Street. A very clever talking parrot, but only knows two words – Miaow and Purr.

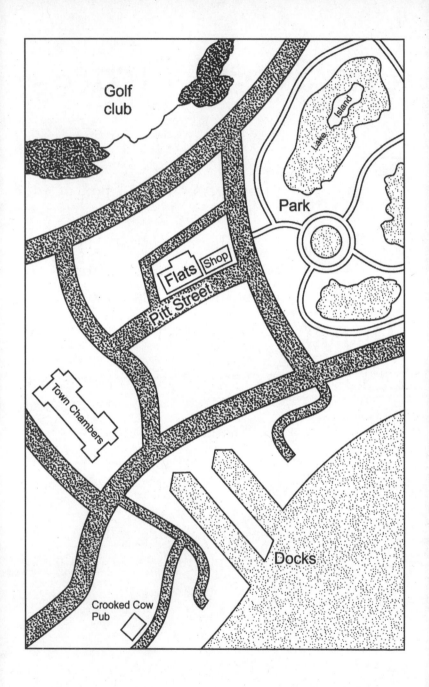

Chapter 1
A Pitt Street Plan

Roger Redbeard didn't have a red beard.

"Why are you called Redbeard then?" Sniffle Smith, his weedy friend, asked ... weedily.

"Because *all* my family are called Redbeard," Roger explained. "Why are you called Sniffle?" he sneered.

"Dunno," Sniffle sniffed. "*Sn-Sn-Sn-iff*! Was your dad called Redbeard?"

Roger scratched his thick, black hair. "I never met my dad," he shrugged.

"So, does your *mum* have a red beard?" Sniffle asked.

Roger sighed. Sometimes Sniffle could be thicker than the doorstep that they sat on. "The Redbeards took their name from the famous Captain Redbeard. He was a great pirate!" Roger said proudly.

"What sort of planes did he fly?" Sniffle asked.

"P-I-R-O-T, you dummy! Pirate! Not *pilot*," Roger moaned. "The terror of the high seas. Robber of Spanish gold."

Sniffle stirred the dust in the gutter with his toe. "I wish we were pirates. I could do with some gold."

Roger glared at the shabby buildings across the street. He half closed his eyes … and saw great ships in his mind. Galleons under full sail. "Why not, Sniffle? Why not?"

"Er … because we haven't got a ship!" Sniffle suggested.

"We'll build one! Mr Clark at the corner shop has stacks of old, wooden boxes! We'll build a ship and sail the seven seas."

"I have to be back in time for supper," Sniffle pointed out.

"Then we'll sail the seven park lakes!" Roger cried and jumped to his feet. He hurried down the street to the corner shop. Sniffle shuffled after him. And following from the shadows came a cat. A moth-eaten, lop-eared, flea-ridden cat. They called her Minnie because it rhymed with Skinny.

Roger Redbeard was the first Redbeard for 400 years to build a pirate ship. And the first one *ever* to build it in his back yard. Sniffle sniffed at the sight of it.

"It'll never float!"

"Hah! That's what they said about the *Titanic* !" Roger scoffed.

"Did they?" asked Sniffle.

"They did! And look what happened to that!" he said.

"I see!" Sniffle smiled – but he didn't see. He still felt unhappy. "Can I be Captain?" he asked.

"You can be Cabin boy," Roger offered. "You can climb to the top of the crow's nest and keep a look out."

"Is that a big job?"

"You can't get any higher," Roger chuckled ... and hit another thumb with the hammer.

After hours of hard work the boat was ready. There was just one problem – or three.

"How do we get it down to the lake?"

"Don't ask stupid questions," Roger replied. "How do they get a ship in a bottle?"

"I don't know," Sniffle had to admit.

"Exactly!" Roger cried.

"But it won't go through the gate!" Sniffle pointed out.

"It came in, didn't it?" Roger sneered.

There was no answer to that. But Sniffle was right.

"Push!" the Captain ordered. Sniffle pushed. Nothing happened. "You push while I pull!" Roger suggested.

The Cabin boy pushed one end while the Captain pulled the same end. Nothing happened. Captain Redbeard scratched his chin – which didn't have a red beard. "What we need is fresh muscles," he said. "And I know just the place to get them!"

"Yeah! You can get fresh mussels down at the fish shop!" Sniffle cried. "And cockles and winkles."

Roger took no notice of him and set off up the steps and along the corridor to Flat 13.

Chapter 2
A Mighty Mate

In Flat 13 Ellie Flynn lay across her bed. It was a king-size bed. Ellie was a big girl. She was reading a book and watching an old black-and-white film. She was clever like that.

Sniffle had trouble doing two things at once – like chewing gum and walking.

Ellie heard the rap at the door. "Come in!" she called.

Roger kicked the door open. *Crack*.

"Roger!" Ellie cried and hugged herself.

"Ouch!" Roger cried and hugged his aching foot.

"You don't know how long I've waited for this moment," she sighed.

"Which moment would that be?" Roger blinked.

"Why, the moment when you walk in here and sweep me off my feet. Of all the bedrooms in all the flats in all of Pitt Street, you walk into mine. What do you want, sweetheart?" she asked gently.

"He wants some fish," Sniffle said.

Roger put his foot carefully on the floor. "I'm Captain Roger Redbeard. I need a little help to launch my new ship," he explained.

Ellie jumped off the bed. The floor creaked. "Oh, you're playing at pirates? Can I join the crew?"

"Not *playing*," Roger said. "And whoever heard of a woman pirate?"

"I have. There's one in the opera, *The Pirates of Penzance*, she's called Ruth," Ellie said at once. She could read *and* listen to opera.

"Well," Roger said smugly, "My crew of pirates are going to be Ruth-*less*. Hee! Hee! Hee! Get it? *Ruth*-less!"

Sniffle laughed. But he didn't know why.

Ellie shrugged. "OK, but then you don't get the boat launched."

"You're in the crew," Roger said quickly. "First mate."

"She could have my job in the cow's nest," Sniffle offered.

"Crow's nest," Roger hissed.

"Whatever."

"No. She wouldn't fit."

Ellie led the way to the door. "*Avast and belay, me hearties*!" she cried. (She'd read the right books.)

"Er, how do I do that?" Sniffle asked.

Roger shrugged and followed her into the yard.

Ellie looked at the ship. "It'll never float," she said sadly.

Sniffle smiled proudly as he remembered what Roger had told him. "That's what they said about the *Titanic*! And look what happened to that!"

"It sank," Ellie said flatly.

There was no answer to that. Sniffle sniffled. *Sn-Sn-Sn-iff*!

Roger looked at her crossly. "And I suppose you're going to say it won't go through the gate," he snapped.

"Yeah," the Cabin boy chipped in. "Well how come they get bottles in ships? Eh?"

Ellie smiled. "Never mind. It'll go *over* the wall." And she picked up the galleon and carried it towards the street. Roger stretched up a hand and rested it under the ship. "OK, Ellie, I've got it!"

Ellie lifted it onto the top of the wall, balanced it there, and ran through the gate to catch it as it slid into the back lane. Shifting it onto her broad shoulders she marched off towards the Pitt Street Park as the Captain, the Cabin boy and the curious cat hurried after her.

Smaller kids rushed to their front doors to look at the wonderful sight. A galleon in full sail down Pitt Street.

"What are you going to call her, Roger?" Mr Clark called as he passed the corner shop.

Roger's mind raced. "Er ... the *Titanic*!" he called.

Mr Clark shook his old head and mumbled into his beard, "Hope there's no icebergs down on the park pond."

There were no icebergs. But there were lots of kids with yachts and motorboats of all shapes and sizes. As the Pitt Street Pirates and the *Titanic* reached the edge of the lake, the kids backed away and ran for the trees as if they'd seen a mad dog. Soon the pond was empty. Ellie slid the ship onto the grass at the edge of the lake.

"How's that, Captain?" she asked.

Roger shrugged. "Not bad. But you didn't have to carry it *all* the way. Sniffle and I could have managed, you know."

"Aye, aye, Captain," the girl said in a humble voice.

Roger Redbeard patted his good ship proudly. "I name this ship *Titanic*. Er ..."

"May God bless her and all who sail in her," Ellie put in.

"I was *coming* to that," Roger snapped. "May dogs get her and all who fail in her!"

And he threw his shoulder against the back of the ship to launch it into the cruel sea.

Sniffle cheered.

Minnie purred.

Ellie clapped.

And Roger cried, "Ouch! My poor shoulder!" as the *Titanic* decided to stay on the shore.

Chapter 3
A Treasure Island

Fifty pairs of curious eyes watched from the bushes in Pitt Street Park as Ellie stepped forward and pushed the galleon gently towards the water. Fifty mouths held their breaths as the *Titanic* hit the water with a splash and a tidal wave that gave the frogs a fright. Fifty kids and Ellie and a cat gasped as the ship bobbed happily up and down on the water.

"It floats!" Ellie breathed.

Roger shrugged his good shoulder and tried not to look too pleased. "'Course! What did you expect?"

"Nothing less, Captain," Ellie grinned. "Shiver me timbers."

"Er ... shiver your what?" asked Roger.

"Me timbers, Captain. That's what all the pirates say," Ellie explained.

"They do?" Roger blinked. He moved closer to her and looked at her properly for the first time. "You seem to know a lot about it."

"I've read all the books, seen all the films. I know all about Long John Silver!" she told him. "And Errol Flynn, the film star, same name as me."

"Uh-huh? Anything else you reckon I should know?"

"Don't worry. I'll tell you everything at the pirate's lair tonight."

"Pirate's *lair*?" Sniffle cut in.

"That's right. My room," Ellie went on happily. "Ship's biscuits and grog!"

"I don't like frogs," Sniffle muttered.

Roger just shook his head. This pirate stuff was a lot harder than he'd thought. "All aboard the *Titanic*!" he cried, and he stepped from the edge of the lake onto the swaying ship.

Sniffle followed and struggled to his post at the top of the mast. The mast was weak and it swayed a bit.

The ship sank a little lower in the water as Ellie joined them with a cry of, "Shiver me timbers!"

Minnie the cat leaped aboard just as Ellie pushed them off from the shore with a piece of wood. She used it to paddle them out into the lake as Roger grabbed the rudder and tried to steer.

Roger half closed his eyes. He could see the seven seas stretching out before the bows. He cried out, "Tiver me shimbers!" He looked up to the top of the mast. "Can you see anything, Mr Cabin Boy?" he cried.

Sniffle pointed back to the shore. "A Spanish galleon, Captain!" he called back.

Roger swung round. There, on the shore, a little girl stood and glared at them. She had the most white and frilly dress Roger had ever seen.

"I say! You people in that boat! Come here at once!" she ordered.

"Turn the ship around and go back, Ellie!" Roger said.

"You mean *avast and belay,* don't you?" the First mate asked.

"Do I?" the dazed Captain Redbeard asked.

"Aye, aye, Sir!" the girl cried and paddled back towards the shore.

Roger stared at the girl who stood there. Her fair hair fell in ringlets to her shoulders and was held with small blue bows. But he wasn't looking at her hair. He was looking at her cycle. A three-wheeled cycle with more golden glitter than a fairy's wand. Shinier than a galleon full of gold.

The *Titanic* crunched into the shore and sent Sniffle tumbling into the lake. "Help! Roger! Help! I can't swim. Help! I'm drowning!" he wailed.

"No you're not," Ellie sighed. "The water's only up to your knees. Stand up, Cabin boy."

Sniffle gave a silly grin and dripped his weedy way to the side of the lake.

"Now," the girl on the golden cycle said. "I want you people to take me out to the island in the middle of the lake."

Roger just stared at her and Sniffle just grinned. Ellie glared. "Why should we?"

The little girl tossed her curls and said, "Because I am Ruby Rose."

"I'm sorry to hear that," Sniffle said.

The girl frowned at him. "My daddy is the mayor of this town. Mayor Rupert Rose. The town golf club is having a special fun day for children. It is my job to sort out the treasure hunt."

"Treasure!" Roger squeaked.

Ruby Rose went on. "I plan to hide a clue on that island in the lake. Now. Take me across in that raft of yours."

"Yes, Miss," Roger said.

"No way," Ellie snapped.

Roger's mouth fell open. "I'm the Captain," he reminded her.

"Sorry, Sir," Ellie whispered. "But we can make some money out of this. Charge her!"

At the magic word Roger's eyes lit up. "Yeah! It'll cost you ten pence ..."

"A pound!" "Ellie said.

"A deal!" Ruby Rose agreed. "I'll pay you when we're safely back."

And they set off across the lake again with the grand Miss Rose aboard.

The Pitt Street Pirates sailed across the lake in silence. They had no choice. Ruby talked so much. "This will be the last clue but one. If they solve this one they'll find the one that tells them where the buried treasure is," she told them. She pulled a slip of paper from her frilly, white handbag and held it under Roger's nose. It said ...

In Pitt Street Park, up a tree
somewhere within THIS LAND I'll be.

"Get it?" Ruby chuckled.

Roger shook his head. "Good!" the girl giggled. "Only the really brainy ones will see the answer."

"Can I look?" Ellie asked. Ellie glanced at the paper then went back to her paddling. "Easy," she said.

Ruby's face turned angry purple. "No it's not! There are hundreds of trees in Pitt Street Park."

"But only one on the island," Ellie said softly.

"How do you know it's on the island?" asked Ruby, pouting her lips.

"The clue says, 'Somewhere within THIS LAND'." Ellie had worked it out. "Take the I-S from THIS and the L-A-N-D and you have I-S-L-A-N-D. Island!"

"Land ahoy!" Sniffle cried.

"Hah!" Ruby Rose sneered. "You only knew that because that's where we're going."

"Land a-hoyyyy!" Sniffle screeched.

"Oh no, I didn't!" Ellie retorted.

"Oh yes, you did!"

"Land a-HOYYYY!!"

"Oh no, I didn't!"

"Oh yes, you ... eeeeek!"

Ccccrrrunnnch! The *Titanic* hit the island.

"Land a-h-e-e-e-e-lp!" Sniffle cried as he sailed from the crow's nest and landed at the top of the island's only tree.

"Abandon ship!" Roger cried as he scrambled ashore.

"You'll be hearing from my daddy's lawyers about *this*!" Ruby cried as green water lapped over her shiny, red shoes.

"Sorry, Captain," Ellie said with a sheepish smile as the *Titanic* sank in the shallow water.

Chapter 4
A Four-Legged Parrot

When Ellie had lifted Sniffle down from the tree, Ruby gave her the treasure hunt clue. "Put that up in the tree!" she ordered.

For once Ellie didn't argue with her. She reached up to the lower branches with her large hand.

Sniffle picked pieces of twig out of his nose and sighed, "How do we get back, Captain Roger?"

Roger was looking sadly at the huge hole in the *Titanic's* bows. "Swim, I suppose," he sighed.

"I can't swim!" Sniffle gasped.

"And I *won't*!" Ruby said and stamped her slimy sock. "I'll just wait here to be rescued by Daddy's helicopter ... but we'll send you the fuel bill," she warned.

"I guess I'll have to carry you back," Ellie said. "The water's not too deep for me."

So Ellie carried Ruby while Roger carried Sniffle. Minnie sat on Sniffle's head. Ruby complained. "Mind you don't splash that smelly water on my best dress! Cost a thousand pounds in Paris, this did! And I don't think much of *your* dress, my dear

Ellie! My servants clean the silver with better rags than that!"

When Ellie reached the shore the rich girl ordered, "Put me down."

Ellie turned and walked back to the edge of the lake. She put Ruby down. She put her down in the deepest, weediest part of the lake she could find.

Ruby came up spitting tadpoles and threats. "You'll be hearing from Daddy's lawyers!" Ruby screeched as the Pitt Street Pirates ran for the safety of the narrow, dusty streets. All they could hear was the wail of the rich girl as she dripped towards her cycle. "Oh, no! Somebody's stolen my hubcaps!"

Roger panted as they ran, "We didn't get that pound off her."

Ellie just grinned. "Never mind. I've got something much better!" She opened her fist and waved a piece of paper under Roger's nose. "I have the last clue to the treasure hunt. Solve the clue and get the prize! Meet me tonight in the pirate's lair!"

****

Later that evening, Ellie Flynn switched off her TV and smiled. "That was Errol Flynn again ... doing what pirates have to do!" she said.

"Just like my Auntie Jane," Sniffle said.

"Your aunt was a pirate?"

"No, but she does what she has to do."

"Shut up, Sniffle," Roger sighed.

"Yes, Captain Roger."

"And what was that song again ... *me hearty*?" young Redbeard asked his mate.

"*Fifteen men on the dead man's chest, Yo-ho-ho and a bottle of rum,*" Ellie said.

Sniffle shook his head. "That song's no good for me, Captain."

"Why not?" demanded Roger.

"I can't count to fifteen. I only have ten fingers."

"You lily-livered land blubber ..." Roger snarled.

"*Lubber!*" Ellie said. "*Land lubber.*"

"Yeah!" Roger nodded. "He's one of those too. I'll have you talking to tanks!"

"*Walking the plank,*" Ellie said gently.

"Yeah, that's it! Walking the plank!" Captain Redbeard turned to Ellie. "Am I starting to sound like Errol Flynn?" he asked.

"Oh, much better," she smiled. "And of course you're *much* better looking!"

"Of course," Roger agreed.

"Now all we need are the clothes," she went on. "I've made a headscarf for Sniffle and me," she said and reached under her bed.

Sniffle sniffed with joy as he saw the bright red, silk squares. "Where did you get the silk?" he gasped.

"Mum's knickers," she said.

"Won't she miss them?"

"Not until it turns a little colder," the girl told him.

"I'm not wearing knickers on my head," Roger objected.

"Oh, no," Ellie said sweetly. "I made *this* for you." And she pulled out a black cardboard hat that fitted Roger's pirate head exactly. "Now you're a real pirate captain," she said.

"Yeah!" the boy said as he tilted his head to one side and looked in the cracked mirror proudly.

He opened his shirt to the waist, kicked off his shoes and strutted proudly across the room. "Are we all ready to go now?"

But Ellie shook her head. "You need a parrot on your shoulder – just like Long John Silver."

"Where will we get a parrot in Pitt Street?" Sniffle asked.

Ellie fixed her eyes on Minnie the cat. Suddenly her long arm shot out and grabbed the cat. With her other hand, she whisked a piece of elastic round Minnie's head and fastened a cardboard beak onto her nose. She dumped the confused cat on Roger's shoulder. "*Now* we are a pirate crew!" she said.

"Without a ship," Sniffle pointed out.

"Ah, but with a treasure chest to find," she reminded him. "Let's work out this clue to Ruby Rose's Treasure Hunt. We'll be able to buy a *hundred* ships by this time tomorrow," she promised.

The treasure is there
if you seek deep down
in the jumbled EARTH
of the MATCHES BROWN

Chapter 5
The Crooked Cow

"I'll read the clue," Ellie said and unfolded the grubby piece of paper which Ruby had given her to put in the tree.

"That's it!" Roger cried. "Matches brown ... matches you can buy in Brown's shop, perhaps."

"I don't think so," Ellie tried to tell him.

But Roger wasn't listening. "Do you know any shops owned by a Mister or Missus Brown?" he asked Sniffle.

Sniffle blinked. "Old Bully Brown runs the *Crooked Cow* pub in Dock Street."

Roger punched the air, "That's it!" Then he punched his Cabin boy on the arm. "Brilliant, Sniffle! Brilliant! Maybe you're not as stupid as you look."

Sniffle was so pleased that he hardly noticed the pain in his arm.

Roger jumped to his feet. "We just have to dig in the earth in the back yard of the *Crooked Cow*!"

"No!" Ellie said. "You don't understand ..."

"Hey!" Sniffle whispered. "That's a pretty tough place! They say that Baby-face Ging's gang used to hang out there in the old days. It was their hideout."

"Scared?" Roger sneered.

"Nope," Sniffle said. "Terrified."

But Roger was heading for the door with a clinging cat on his shoulder. Ellie grabbed Sniffle's hand and hurried after him. "Why would Ruby Rose want to plant treasure down that part of town?" she tried to argue.

Roger grabbed a garden trowel from Mrs Taylor's window box as he hurried out into the cool night air. "The clue is in the word *jumbled*, Roger!" the girl tried to tell him. "It means the letters are all mixed up to make another word."

But Roger wasn't listening. Pitt Street was a sea of shadows between pools of pale lamplight. The Captain sailed on with his two helpers trailing in his wake.

"You see," Ellie was saying, "mix up the letters in BROWN MATCHES to make new words and you get TOWN CHAMBERS. That's where the town council meets. That's where a girl like Ruby Rose would hide the treasure. You understand, Sniffle, don't you?"

"Er ... no, Ellie."

But Ellie went on. "The letters E-A-R-T-H can be changed to make HEART. And B-R-O-W-N M-A-T-C-H-E-S means *heart* of the *Town Chambers*. See?"

"Er ... no, Ellie."

"The treasure's in the Council Chamber!" she told them.

Sniffle shook his head. "Captain Roger was right about the *Titanic*," he told her. "I guess he's right this time too."

"Yes," she sighed. "He's a wonderful Captain and a brilliant ship-builder ... but he's just rotten at word games!"

Still Roger rushed on down the mean streets muttering, "*Avast and belay there me hearties. Pieces of eight and Spanish gold!*" The tooting of the tug boats broke the silence of the dark alleys as they neared the old dock area of the town. The damp river air made Ellie shiver.

The shapes in the shadows made Sniffle tremble.

But bold Roger Redbeard raced on with dreams of gold to keep out the cold.

At last he reached the high back wall of the *Crooked Cow* pub.

Chapter 6
Hello Ello

Minnie the cat fell from his shoulder as Roger scrambled to climb the two-metre brick wall. Ellie came behind him and whispered, "Let me help you, Captain!"

She cupped her hands, Roger placed one foot in them and she lifted ... a little too quickly. Roger shot over the wall like a pirate's cannonball and landed in the yard on his head.

He shook himself and listened. Faint sounds of harsh laughter spilled out from the old bar. A tomcat howled in a nearby alley. Minnie, the ship's parrot, howled back.

But closer still someone stirred in the shadows by the gate. "Who's that there?" the bold pirate Captain hissed.

"Who's that *there*?" a trembling reply came.

"Who's that there, saying, 'Who's that there?'"

"Who's that there, saying, 'Who's that there, saying, who's that there?'" the creaking voice croaked.

"I asked first," Roger Redbeard said. "Who are you?"

"Not telling," came the voice, followed by a soft, "*Sn-sn-sn-iff*!"

"Sniffle?" Roger gasped. "How did you get in here?"

"Through the gate," the Cabin boy replied. "It's open you know."

Roger sighed. Sometimes a pirate's life is not an easy one. "Let Ellie in," he ordered and began scratching at the hard earth in the corner. "You two find your own patch and let me know if you find anything."

After half an hour Roger was up to his shoulders in the hole. He'd hit solid rock. He looked out stiffly. The yard was quiet. "Ellie?"

"Aye aye, Captain?"

"Found anything?"

"Twenty-three worms and half a dozen dog bones."

"Sniffle?"

"*Sn-sn-sn-iff?*"

"Found anything?"

"Nah. Just an old suitcase."

"A suitcase!" the Captain cried. "What's in it? Gold and silver? Emeralds and diamonds?"

"No-o. Nothing like that sort of stuff. It's full of paper. Looks like five pound notes!"

"Treasure!" Ellie and her Captain cried together. They slammed the suitcase shut, snatched it up and rushed out into the alley. They also rushed out into the arms of the waiting policeman.

"Now, what would we be having here?" P.C. Ello asked and took the suitcase gently from the pirate Captain's hands. "Had a report of noises in the pub's backyard. Landlord was worried! I came around to find out what was going on. You kids should be in bed at this time of night anyway."

The policeman fiddled with the catches of the old suitcase and the lid burst open. Piles of banknotes tumbled to the ground and the old policeman whistled, "And where would you be getting this sort of money?"

"In the backyard of the *Crooked Cow* bar," Ellie said sadly. "Captain, I mean Roger, worked out it would be there."

"He did now, did he?" the policeman grinned. "Well he's cleverer than all the town's police! We've been looking for Baby-face Ging's loot for 25 years and have never found it."

"This is Ruby Rose's Treasure Hunt treasure," Sniffle said.

Officer Ello laughed, "Nah! That's in the heart of the town Council Chamber ... everybody knows that! All the golf club kids will end up there tomorrow, I reckon. No. this is Baby-face Ging's treasure all right. And you found it. You know what this means?"

Roger sighed. He was tired. It had been a bad day. "Trouble," was all he could say.

"Hah! No, me boy! More like a reward!" the policeman chuckled. "I'll just look after these old banknotes for you ... they're *old* notes so they ain't worth nothing nowadays. You call at the Council Chamber tomorrow afternoon and I'll bet the mayor will have some great reward for you."

The policeman stuffed the money back in the case, picked it up and plodded off down the alley.

The pale streetlights glinted in Ellie's adoring eyes. "Oh, Roger," she said. "You are wonderful!"

Even in the dark Roger's cheeks glowed red. "Am I better than Errol Flynn?" he asked.

"Much better," said Ellie sweetly.

"Even better than my Aunt Jane!" Sniffle agreed.

"*Avast, me hearties!*" roared Roger. "We'll meet tomorrow in the Council Chamber."

Chapter 7
Paper Pounds

Mayor Rupert Rose polished his glasses and blinked. He cleared his throat which was as thin as a chicken's. "And now that the council business is finished," he said, "it is my great pleasure to present the prizes to the finders of the treasure!"

He stroked his chin. Then he took an envelope out of his pocket. "In this envelope there are two tickets to America ..."

"Oh, Roger," Ellie crooned. "You and I can go away together."

The pirate Captain looked a little unhappy. "Wouldn't you rather take Sniffle?" he asked.

Ellie punched him playfully on the arm as Mayor Rupert Rose went on, "Would the winners of the treasure hunt please step forward?"

Minnie wobbled on Captain Roger's shoulder as he stepped onto the floor of the Council Hall. The councillors gasped. Suddenly the council clerk whispered in the mayor's ear.

The mayor blinked and coughed again. "There seems to have been some mistake! The children you see before you are in *fact* the finders of Baby-face Ging's treasure, not the winners of the treasure hunt!"

"Ahhhh!" the councillors sighed.

The mayor reached under the table and pulled out the suitcase the pirates had found. "Of course the loot is worthless now. You can have it all back. But we'd also like to give you a token of the town's thanks!" He pushed a chest at Roger and turned to the clerk. "Now," he said with a sour smile, "Where are my Rose and the real treasure hunt winners?"

The clerk turned red and muttered in the mayor's ear as the Pitt Street Pirates were shown out of the Council Chamber in a hurry.

Roger stood in the bright heat of the street a little dazed. "Open the chest, Captain Roger," Sniffle said.

Roger opened it and looked inside. He stared. Ellie reached forward and took something out of the chest.

"What is it? Gold? Jewels? More holiday tickets?"

Roger shook his head. Ellie held a roll of paper. She unrolled it and read ...

The Town Council wishes to express its thanks to Roger Redwood and friends for finding the Ging Gang goodies.

Signed

Rupert Rose (Mayor)

"They couldn't even get my name right," Roger said and trailed sadly back to Pitt Street.

"Is that all?" Sniffle wanted to know.

"There are a thousand of those useless old £5 notes. They aren't worth a penny!" Roger sighed.

"Will we build another *Titanic*?" Sniffle asked Roger as they walked past Mr Clark's shop.

The Captain of the sunken ship just stared gloomily at the gutter.

"Cheer up," Ellie said. "It could be worse."

The boy looked at her. "How? I'm a pirate who never stole anything. My buried treasure is not worth a penny. I'm a loser. How could I be worse?"

"You could be Ruby Rose!" Ellie grinned and nodded to the end of the street.

A three-wheeled, gold and silver-plated cycle came round the corner on just two of its three wheels. Ruby Rose's legs were a blur and her ribbons streamed behind her in a wild tangle. "Help! Oh! Help!" she cried. "They want to kill me!"

"What's wrong, Ruby?" Ellie asked ... as if she didn't know.

"The golf club kids have worked all day to follow up the clues – they went wild when they had to wade across the Pitt Street Park lake in their best clothes," the rich girl gasped and looked over her shoulder in panic.

"It's worth it for the treasure," Roger shrugged.

"Yes! But when they got across the lake they found the clue had gone! And now they're blaming me!" she wailed.

"So how did they know where the treasure was if they never found the clue?" asked Ellie.

"PC Ello told them. But they're still mad at me," Ruby replied.

"She's here!" a voice called out. A group of dripping, muddy, angry, rich kids charged round the corner and set off screaming after Ruby Rose.

"Wahhhh!" she sobbed. "They said they're going to throw me in!"

"You'll float," the Captain laughed – the first time he'd laughed for an hour.

"I won't float with this bike wrapped round my neck!" she shouted as she pedalled down the pot-holed road. "Oh, I wish I hadn't lost my hubcaps!"

The wild and red-faced golf club kids vanished round the corner after Ruby. Roger Redbeard rolled about on the front doorstep with laughter. Even Sniffle saw the joke.

Ellie shrugged and waved a grubby piece of paper with the treasure hunt clue. "I think that this is what you lost!" she giggled. "Hey, Captain! Who said we couldn't rob the rich?"

"Robbing is wrong!" a creaking old voice said from the shop doorway. They were standing by the dusty windows of Mr Clark's shop and it was the old shopkeeper speaking.

The man shuffled to the door. "What have you got there, then?" he asked.

Roger showed him what was in the suitcase. "Old £5 notes," he sighed. "Worthless!"

Mr Clark looked in the box and shook his head. "Don't be daft, lad! People collect old banknotes like those! They may not be worth £5 each but they are worth something!"

"How much?" Sniffle asked.

"A pound at least!" the old man said. "I'll give you that!"

Roger looked at Ellie and she shrugged. "A pound's better than nothing."

The old man took the suitcase and went back into the gloomy shop. He came out five minutes later with a fat envelope. "Here you are – there were a thousand notes in there – so here's a thousand pounds!"

Roger's mouth opened and closed a dozen times before he could speak. "I thought you said one pound!" he squeaked.

"One pound for each note – a thousand notes, a thousand pounds!" he smiled and shuffled back into the shop. The three pirates wandered down Pitt Street like sleepwalkers.

It was sunset before they woke up in the real world.

Roger sat on the warm doorstep and half-closed his eyes. The old, brown buildings blurred and in his mind he saw great galleons. "We'll build that new galleon. We'll sail the seven seas and bring back Spanish gold!"

"What will you spend your share of the treasure on?" Ellie asked Sniffle.

"A bike," Sniffle said firmly. "And you?"

"A new collar for Minnie, of course," she said stroking the pirate cat till it purred

like a Rolls Royce engine. "Then there are one or two videos I want to watch," Ellie said watching Roger's face.

"Pirate films?"

Ellie shook her head. "Romantic films," she said shyly. "I thought Roger might like to come and watch them with me. Roger?" She nudged him with her elbow.

Roger was looking across the street and seeing the great galleons in his mind. "I'll buy a new ship – a real sailing ship. It'll be the best on the seven seas."

"What'll you call it?" the girl asked. "You could call it the *Fair Ellie*."

Roger frowned. "No-o," he said slowly. "The first ship led us to the treasure, in a way. I guess it was good for us. Yes. I'll call my new ship *Titanic Two* ... I can't help thinking that's a *lucky* name for a ship!"

Barrington Stoke was a famous and much-loved story-teller. He travelled from village to village carrying a lantern to light his way. He arrived as it grew dark and when the young boys and girls of the village saw the glow of his lantern, they hurried to the central meeting place. They were full of excitement and expectation, for his stories were always wonderful.

Then Barrington Stoke set down his lantern. In the flickering light the listeners were enthralled by his tales of adventure, horror and mystery. He knew exactly what they liked best and he loved telling a good story. And another. And then another. When the lantern burned low and dawn was nearly breaking, he slipped away. He was gone by morning, only to appear the next day in some other village to tell the next story.

Barrington Stoke would like to thank all its readers for commenting on the manuscript before publication and in particular:

Rachel Barclay
Jenny Blues
Kirsty Bosher
Matthew Burger
Kenneth Burns
Peter Carpenter
Sarah Creates
Robert Critcher
Harriet Curson
Linda Darroch
Adam Garrett
Rebecca Grantham
Alexander Hatzidakis

Rosemary Henderson
Yvonne Keeping
Hetty Malik
Harriet Maxwell
Isabel Mercer
Richard Nicholls
Jason Nickerson
Emily Pearson
Katie Shuttleworth
James Stubbs
Lorna Studholme
Christopher Tuck
Nikolas Ward

Become a Consultant!

Would you like to give us feedback on our titles before they are published? Contact us at the email address below – we'd love to hear from you!

Email: info@barringtonstoke.co.uk
Website: www.barringtonstoke.co.uk

If you loved this story, why don't you read . . .

Ghost for Sale

by Terry Deary

Would you like to see a ghost?
Mr and Mrs Rundle buy a haunted
wardrobe to attract more customers to
their inn, but the result is not quite what
they expect.

You can order *Ghost for Sale* directly from our
website at www.barringtonstoke.co.uk

If you loved this story, why don't you read . . .

The Hat Trick

by Terry Deary

Is there something you'll remember for as long as you'll live? Seaburn football team meet their rivals and Jud has to step in as goalie. They are two goals down at half-time. How can Seaburn recover?